HOPE FOR HAITI

Jesse Joshua Watson

G. P. PUTNAM'S SONS

AN IMPRINT OF PENGUIN GROUP (USA) INC.

For the resilient youth of Haiti.
May they find their footing and
finally be given the chance to run a fair race.

For those people across the world who have joined together in support of Haiti.
May we not let our brothers and sisters slip from our attention
but press on to rebuild a Haiti that is secure and prosperous.

For Rubin Pfeffer, a sage inspirer.

And a very special thank you to my models, who brought this book to life.

G. P. PUTNAM'S SONS

A division of Penguin Young Readers Group.
Published by The Penguin Group. Penguin Group (USA) Inc., 375 Hudson Street, New York, NY 10014, U.S.A. Penguin Group (Canada), 90 Eglinton Avenue East, Suite 700, Toronto, Ontario M4P 2Y3, Canada (a division of Pearson Penguin Canada Inc.). Penguin Books Ltd, 80 Strand, London WC2R 0RL, England. Penguin Ireland, 25 St. Stephen's Green, Dublin 2, Ireland (a division of Penguin Books Ltd.). Penguin Group (Australia), 250 Camberwell Road, Camberwell, Victoria 3124, Australia (a division of Pearson Australia Group Pty Ltd). Penguin Books India Pvt Ltd, 11 Community Centre, Panchsheel Park, New Delhi - 110 017, India. Penguin Group (NZ), 67 Apollo Drive, Rosedale, North Shore 0632, New Zealand (a division of Pearson New Zealand Ltd). Penguin Books (South Africa) (Pty) Ltd, 24 Sturdee Avenue, Rosebank, Johannesburg 2196, South Africa. Penguin Books Ltd, Registered Offices: 80 Strand, London WC2R 0RL, England.

Published simultaneously in Canada. Printed in the United States of America.
Design by Ryan Thomann. Text set in Chaparral Semibold.
The art was done in acrylic on Strathmore 500 series illustration board.

Library of Congress Cataloging-in-Publication Data
Watson, Jesse Joshua. Hope for Haiti / Jesse Joshua Watson. p. cm. Summary: A young boy finds hope when he is given an old soccer ball to play with in the wake of Haiti's devastating earthquake. 1. Haiti Earthquake, Haiti, 2010—Juvenile fiction. [1. Haiti Earthquake, Haiti, 2010—Fiction. 2. Earthquakes—Haiti—Fiction. 3. Soccer—Fiction. 4. Haiti—Fiction.] I. Title. PZ7.W32747Ho 2010 [E]—dc22
2010006835
ISBN 978-0-399-25547-2
1 3 5 7 9 10 8 6 4 2

AUTHOR'S NOTE

When I was young, my father worked as a designer for the humanitarian aid organization World Vision International. He brought home photos of kids from poverty-stricken countries, and specifically Haiti. I spent my childhood wishing there was something I could do to ease the people's suffering. As I got older, I saw how my own country was further impoverishing Haiti with its economic and political policies. Then, when the earthquake hit, I felt void of hope . . . until I started seeing photos of children playing soccer amidst the chaos. And in this I found great hope for Haiti, that even in the most tragic of circumstances, children are resilient and will overcome. This is the hope I want to share with children everywhere. —J.J.W.

When the earth shook and took away my neighborhood, I thought I would never be happy again.

Wailing filled my ears.

Dust filled my nose.

Tears filled my eyes.

I helped my mother build

a new home in the soccer stadium.

One piece of tin.

Six posts.

Three sheets.

Many people have come here to make shelters. Some kids wander around lost or wait in line for water.

I am too small to compete for the food that the Blue Hats are passing out, so I sit and watch strangers speaking different languages quickly pass boxes toward the front of the line.

In my new neighborhood,
people lie in the shade of tarps,
many of them injured. When I see
a girl kicking a ball made of rags,
I remember how we used to be happy
playing before the quake.

"Can I play?" I ask.

"Sure," she says.

We juggle the ball, trying to keep it off the ground.

Other kids come running to join us. Now we have a game.

I forget about my hunger as I dribble the ball through two defenders and pass it to a teammate.

We keep the ball moving quickly between us, like a dance.

I shoot the ball between two piles of sandals and jump into the arms of my teammates, like I've seen them do on TV.

Both teams burst into laughter until an old woman shushes us as she passes.

"This is no time to laugh," she scolds. "There is too much sadness here."

As she walks away, a man nearby says, "Don't worry, children. It's not your fault. She has much to mourn. And she does not understand the power of this game."

The man grins and starts dribbling our ball. "So, any of you been to a game in this stadium?"

Several children nod. I smile and say, "My father took me to a match here. We had a picnic with green papaya salad, and he bought me a soda. Seeing those players made me want to be a soccer star when I grow up."

"I remember watching Manno Sanon, Haiti's most famous soccer player, score goals on this very field," the man says. "He was just a city kid like you. No different."

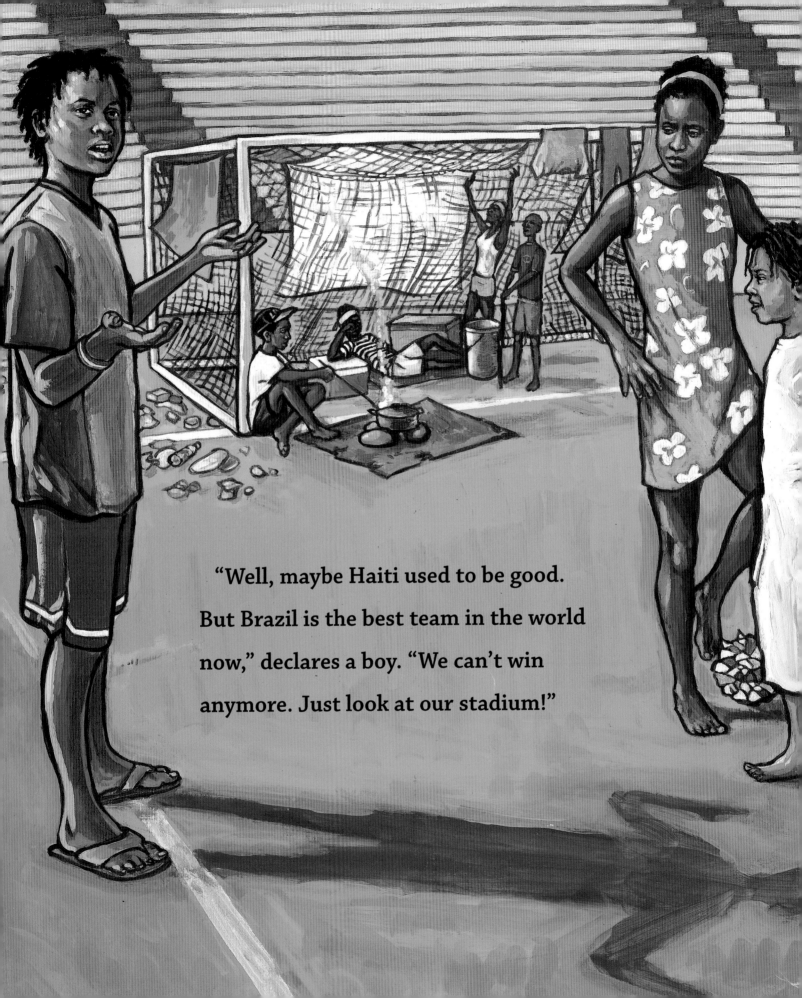

"Well, maybe Haiti used to be good. But Brazil is the best team in the world now," declares a boy. "We can't win anymore. Just look at our stadium!"

The man picks up our rag ball

and tries juggling it on his knees.

The rags are soaked with mud and keep slipping

from the rubber bands that hold them together.

"Listen. I must get back to help the others," he says. "But before I go, I would like to give you kids something."

He ducks into his shelter. When he comes back out, he is carrying a ball.
A real soccer ball.

He hands it to me and turns to go. It is an old ball but in perfect condition. There is a signature written on the ball, but I can't read it.

A boy looks closely. "It says Manno Sanon!"

All of the kids gather close to see.

"Wait," I call. "You can't give this ball away. It's signed by Manno!"

"We can let go of the past," the man tells us. "Right now we need to think about the future. And the future is you."

I put my arms around the man, and the other kids all swarm him with hugs.

"Thank you, mister," we all say.

"Don't thank me, children," he says. "Thank you. Thank you for reminding me why there is hope for Haiti."

We return to our game, playing better than ever.

I pass the ball to my teammate, who traps it with his chest,

then flicks it over the head of a defender.

As I run for the ball, I am no longer barefoot and wearing torn shorts. I am wearing the Haitian uniform and the stadium is packed with fans screaming out my name.

I beat the defender to the ball, spin around and glance at the net. With the Brazilian team racing toward me, I take one more step . . .

. . . shoot and . . .

...*GOAL!*